D0328298

SCHOLASTIC INC.
New York Toronto London Auckland
Sydney Mexico City New Delhi Hong Kong

No part of this work may be reproduced in whole or in part, or stored in a retrieval system, or transmitted in any form or by any means, electronic, mechanical, photocopying, recording, or otherwise, without written permission of the publisher. For information regarding permission, write to Scholastic Inc., Attention: Permissions Department, 557 Broadway, New York, NY 10012.

ISBN: 978-0-545-17725-2

© 2010 Pokémon. © 1997-2010 Nintendo, Creatures, GAME FREAK, TV Tokyo, ShoPro, JR Kikaku. Pokémon properties are trademarks of Nintendo. All rights reserved.
Published by Scholastic Inc.
SCHOLASTIC and associated logos are trademarks and/or registered trademarks of Scholastic Inc.

12 11 10 9 8 7 6 5 4 3 2 1 10 11 12 13 14 15/0

Designed by Henry Ng
Printed in the U.S.A. 40
First printing, January 2010

One sunny day, Ash, Brock, Dawn, and their Pokémon were in the park. Brock was reading the newspaper.

"Wow! The Scarf Monster is in Solaceon Town," Brock said.

The three friends were heading to Solaceon Town to their friend Angie's Pokémon day care center. Until . . .

"Piplup, pip!" Piplup cried.

Something big was crashing through the trees.

"Come on!" Ash exclaimed.

But the creature had disappeared.

"I guess our eyes were playing tricks on us," Ash said.

"Hey, isn't that Angie's house?" asked Dawn.

The door opened. "It's great to see you guys again!" Angie said. "Come on in!"

Angie's parents were on vacation. She and her Shinx had the place to themselves.

"Have you heard about the Scarf Monster?" Ash asked Angie. "We saw it on the way here!"

"Not again!" cried Angie. "I'll be right back!" She dashed out the door.

Ash, Dawn, and Brock followed Angie through the woods and into a cave.

"The Scarf Monster you saw is a Pokémon I'm raising," Angie told them.

Angie left a big bowl of yummy Poké food out for her Pokémon.

The kids hid behind the bushes to wait for it.

"I think I hear something coming!" Angie said.

A big pink tongue reached for the Poké food.

"It's the Scarf Monster!" Dawn yelled.

"No, it's a Lickilicky!" said Brock.

"Your Lickilicky is the Scarf Monster?" Ash asked Angie.

"Yes," said Angie. "I was looking after a Lickitung while its trainer is away. But while we were training, it evolved!"

"It's never a good thing when a caretaker evolves someone else's Pokémon," said Brock.

"Lickilicky hates being in its Poké Ball," Angie went on. "I've been keeping it in this cave so my mom and dad don't find out what happened."

"But why is Lickilicky wearing that scarf?" asked Dawn.

"Lickilicky is not the smallest Pokémon. So I blow up its collar and pull it around like a balloon," Angie explained.

The kids didn't realize it, but Team Rocket was tracking the Scarf Monster, too. They were in disguise.

"We're reporters for the *Sinnoh Star*," Jessie told Ash and Angie. "Can you help us find the Scarf Monster?"

"Sure!" said Ash. "The Scarf Monster's over there." He and Angie pointed in different directions.

"That's strange even for them," James whispered.

The kids met back in the cave.

Angie tied Lickilicky to a rock with a long rope. "Sorry, Lickilicky," she said. "You have to lie low for a while."

The next morning, Lickilicky smelled something sweet in the air — Poké food!

"Mmm. Lickilicky!" it said.

It broke the rope and followed the smell into the woods.

A giant ball of Poké food was waiting for Lickilicky.

Behind the tasty treat was one of Team Rocket's robots!

"The Scarf Monster is falling for our trap!" cried James.

Team Rocket's robot tied up Lickilicky.

"Liiiiicky!" it cried out.

Ash, Brock, Dawn, and Angie found Lickilicky just in time.

"Knock it off! That's Angie's Lickilicky, not yours!" shouted Ash.

"Is that a twerp I hear?" Jessie said.

"This robot can handle those guys, have no fear," Meowth replied.

"That's what you think!" Ash cried.

Pikachu slammed them with Iron Tail. *Pow!*

Shinx snuck in with Quick Attack. *Wham!*

Piplup poked them with Peck. *Pop!*

But the battle had just begun.

"Angie, take care of Lickilicky while we distract Team Rocket!" Brock suggested.

"Great idea!" Angie said.

She and Ash untied Lickilicky.

"Okay, let's get out of here!" Brock yelped.

"Not so fast!" Meowth sneered.

Team Rocket's robot was ready to hurl a giant rock at them.

"Quick, Lickilicky, use Roll Out!" Angie screamed.

Bam! Lickilicky knocked over Team Rocket's robot.

"Awesome!" Angie cried. "Follow it up with Wrap!"

Thwap! Lickilicky tied Team Rocket up with its tongue.

"Pikachu, you know what to do!" called Ash.

"Pikaaaachuuuuu!" Pikachu zapped Team Rocket with Thunderbolt.

"We're blasting off again!" Team Rocket sighed as they flew through the air.

"Great work, buddy! Now let's go home," Angie said.

"You've done a great job raising Lickilicky, Angie!" Ash said.

"Thanks," said Angie. "But how am I going to explain Lickilicky to my mom and dad?"

"Let's tell them together," Ash said.

"I'm so sorry!" Angie told her parents.

"We understand," Angie's mom said. "Lickilicky's trainer will be here soon. You can tell him what happened."

Just then, they heard voices outside the window.

"Wowee, look at my beautiful Lickilicky!" the trainer exclaimed.

"The trainer isn't upset that Lickitung evolved. He's thrilled!" said Dawn.

Angie was grateful to her pals for all their help. "Thanks, guys!"

"That's what friends are for!" said Ash.